ZORRO
GETS AN OUTFIT

CARTER GOODRICH

SIMON & SCHUSTER BOOKS FOR YOUNG READERS

New York   London   Toronto   Sydney   New Delhi

For Sabina, with tenderness, gratitude, and love

SIMON & SCHUSTER BOOKS FOR YOUNG READERS * An imprint of Simon & Schuster Children's Publishing Division * 1230 Avenue of the Americas, New York, New York 10020 * Copyright © 2012 by Carter Goodrich * All rights reserved, including the right of reproduction in whole or in part in any form. * SIMON & SCHUSTER BOOKS FOR YOUNG READERS is a trademark of Simon & Schuster, Inc. * For information about special discounts for bulk purchases, please contact Simon & Schuster Special Sales at 1-866-506-1949 or business@simonandschuster.com. * The Simon & Schuster Speakers Bureau can bring authors to your live event. For more information or to book an event, contact the Simon & Schuster Speakers Bureau at 1-866-248-3049 or visit our website at www.simonspeakers.com. * Book design by Dan Potash * The text for this book is set in Gorey. * The illustrations for this book are rendered in watercolor. * Manufactured in China. * 0212 SCP * 10 9 8 7 6 5 4 3 2 1 Library of Congress Cataloging-in-Publication Data * Goodrich, Carter. * Zorro gets an outfit / Carter Goodrich. – 1st ed. * p. cm. * Summary: Zorro is embarrassed at having to wear a fancy outfit to the park and Mister Bud is unable to cheer him up until a "cool" new dog arrives in his own fancy clothes and challenges the friends to a race. * ISBN 978-1-4424-3535-3 (hardcover : alk. paper) * 1. Dogs–Fiction. 2. Clothing and dress–Fiction. I. Title. * PZ7.G61447Zor 2012 * [E]–dc23 * 2011029153 * ISBN 978-1-4424-3536-0 (eBook)

The day began like any other for Zorro and Mister Bud.

"Okay . . . all right."

THEY HAD THEIR BISCUITS AND
WERE READY FOR THEIR WALK.

BUT THERE WAS A DELAY.

"Look, your very own outfit!"

Let's see if it fits!"

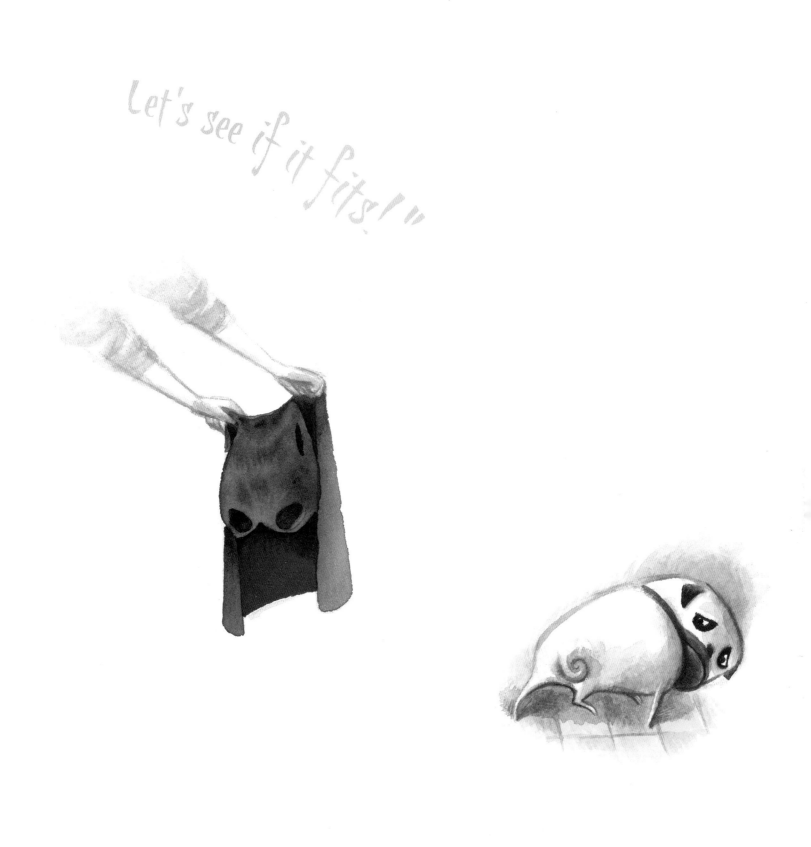

ZORRO WAS EMBARRASSED.

HE DIDN'T WANT TO GO FOR A WALK.

EDDIE AND THE BOYS ALL LAUGHED AT ZORRO.

EVEN SLIM MADE FUN OF HIM.

LOOK! THERE'S SLIM!
LET'S GET HIM!

IN THE PARK MISTER BUD TRIED TO CHEER UP ZORRO.

BUT IT DIDN'T WORK.

SUDDENLY SOMEONE NEW SHOWED UP.

HE WAS FAST!

HE DID AMAZING TRICKS!

AND HE HAD AN OUTFIT . . .

... JUST LIKE ZORRO.

SO THEY RACED.

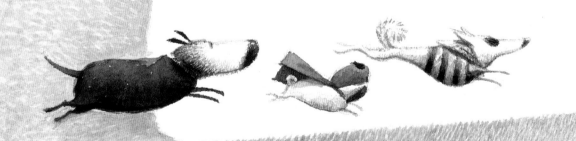

IN THE END DART WON,

ZORRO CAME IN SECOND,

AND MISTER BUD CAME IN THIRD.

PRETTY SOON IT WAS TIME TO GO.

ON THE WAY HOME ZORRO TRIED TO CHEER
UP MISTER BUD ABOUT COMING IN THIRD.

MAYBE IT'S BECAUSE
YOU DON'T HAVE AN
OUTFIT!

ACTUALLY, MISTER BUD DIDN'T REALLY
MIND ABOUT COMING IN THIRD.

HE COULD TELL ZORRO WAS HAPPY NOW.

AND THAT MADE MISTER BUD HAPPY TOO.